B&T 17.99

D0498321

B&T 17.99

Duck and Hippo
GIVE THANKS

By **JONATHAN LONDON**   Illustrated by **ANDREW JOYNER**

two lions

For Sean & Steph, Aaron, and sweet Maureen
—J. L.

For Mum and Dad, with love and thanks
—A. J.

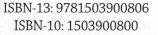

Published by Two Lions, New York

www.apub.com

Amazon, the Amazon logo, and Two Lions are trademarks of Amazon.com, Inc., or its affiliates.

ISBN-13: 9781503900806
ISBN-10: 1503900800

The illustrations are rendered in brush and ink with wash and pencil and then digitally colored.
Series design by Abby Dening
Book design by AndWorld Design

Printed in China
First Edition
1 3 5 7 9 10 8 6 4 2

It was almost Thanksgiving,
and the leaves were still tumbling.

SCRITCH!

SCRITCH!   SCRITCH!

Hippo was raking the leaves into a huge pile
and dreaming of a good, old-fashioned Thanksgiving.

A white blur flew through the air . . .

WHEEEEEEE!

PLOOF!

and plopped right into the middle
of Hippo's pile. What was it?

A head popped up.
It was Duck!

"Duck! Duck!"
cried Hippo.
"What are you *doing?*"

"I'm jumping into a pile of leaves!" said Duck.
"It's *fun!* Why don't you try it?"

"I'm *trying* to make the pile all nice and tidy!"
Hippo said with a huff.

BONK!

Just then an apple fell on Hippo's head.

Hippo rubbed his head, polished the apple,

and handed it to Duck. "For *you!*" he said.

"Thanks, Hippo!" Duck said.

"Speaking of giving thanks," said Hippo, "tomorrow is Thanksgiving. Let's celebrate *together!*"

"YES!" said Duck. "I'll help! And let's invite all our friends!"

To get ready for the feast,
Duck and Hippo
went shopping.

Duck said, "I want to ride in the basket!"
She grabbed food as they zoomed down the aisles.

WHEEEEE!

"*Faster!*"
squealed Duck.

URGH!
URGH!

Then Duck jumped out, and Hippo **squeeezed** in. *But the shopping cart wouldn't budge. And when Hippo tried to squeeeze out . . .*

"I'M STUCK!" cried Hippo.
"NO PROBLEM!"
boomed Elephant.
He lifted Hippo out!

"Thank you, Elephant!" said Duck and Hippo. And Duck invited him for Thanksgiving.
"*DEE*-LIGHTED!"
boomed Elephant.

Hippo wanted some crusty bread for their good, old-fashioned
Thanksgiving. So Duck and Hippo got in line at the bakery.
Turtle was ahead of them.

"You go first," said Turtle. "And take your time. Take your time."

"Thank you, Turtle!" said Duck and Hippo.
And Duck invited him for Thanksgiving.
"Terrific!" said Turtle.

By now, Duck and Hippo were *so* hungry. They went to Pig's Pizza, and they each ate a slice of Pig's special pizza of the day.

"Thank you, Pig!" said Duck and Hippo. And Duck invited her for Thanksgiving. *"Yummy!"* cried Pig. "I can't wait!"

Back at Hippo's house,
Hippo said,
"Oh, there's so much to *do*
for our good, old-fashioned
Thanksgiving!"

So Duck went out and gathered leaves.
She just couldn't help jumping in!

WHEEEEEEEE!

Hippo went out and gathered pumpkins. **"*Quack-a-doodle-doo!*"** cried Duck, sitting on a pumpkin. "I laid an *egg*!"

Then Duck gathered acorn squashes. "Let me help you, Duck," said Hippo.

Lastly, Duck and Hippo gathered apples and headed back inside.

But they bumped into each
other at the door.

"WHOOPS!"

Hippo bowed and said,
"After you, dear Duck!"

Then, together, they decorated the table
with leaves and squashes
and perfect little pumpkins.

When they were done, Duck did a dance
on the tabletop and sang, "TA-DA!"

"See you tomorrow!" she said, jumping off.

That night, Hippo went to sleep and dreamed of a good, old-fashioned Thanksgiving.

Before Duck went to bed, she told their friends,
"Let's make something *special* for Hippo!"

The next day
Hippo was busy.

He baked a
good, old-fashioned
apple pie; and a
good, old-fashioned
pumpkin pie; and a
good, old-fashioned acorn squash.

And his house filled with a
good, old-fashioned smell.

He couldn't wait for his
good, old-fashioned Thanksgiving
to begin!

But it was getting late.
Hippo looked out the window.

The full harvest moon
was rising over the trees.

Night had come.
But where, OH WHERE, were Hippo's friends?

"*Here we are!*" cried Duck,
and they all piled into Hippo's house.

"Sorry we're late! But we were all
finishing up a special *surprise* for you!"

I wonder what it could be? thought Hippo.

Hippo's friends each had something to offer:

Turtle brought
Chinese egg rolls.

Elephant brought
sea-cucumber sushi.

Pig brought pizza napoletana.

And Duck brought
peanut-butter-and-jelly tacos.

"SURPRISE!"

This is NOT a good, old-fashioned Thanksgiving feast! thought Hippo.

But then he looked at the smiling
faces of all his dear friends.

He spread his arms wide and said,
"WELCOME!
And thank you for being who you are!"

"HURRAY!"
everyone shouted.

Then they all gathered around the table and held hands.

Duck and Hippo gave thanks for their friends,
for being together, and for sharing nature's bounty.
"Let's EAT!" cried Pig.

And it was a big, happy Thanksgiving feast—
the best Thanksgiving EVER!

When they were done, Duck said,
"And now, let's go outside . . ."

"... and jump in the leaves!"

WHEEEEE!